Mr. Banks

A. Gavin

Contents

Previously in Sex & Cigarettes

"Bring your ass over here," he commanded.

I obeyed.

"You got me smellin' like sex and cigarettes."

Mayan eased me down on his hard dick, filling me up once again. I shivered when his lips grazed my hardened nipples. I wanted nothing more than to have this feeling forever. My mouth fell open slightly as he slowly lifted me up and down.

"Mayan," I whispered softly.

"Talk to me, Amor," he coached. "You want me to stop?"

"No!" I damn near yelled. "No, please don't stop."

Mayan is the drug and I'm the fiend. I wanted hit after hit. I wanted to feel *him* pumping through my veins, taking me to unimaginable heights.

"Open your eyes and look at me," he demanded.

I allowed my eyes to connect with the man who had my heart in a chokehold. Those piercing brown eyes set my soul on fire. He stuck out his tongue and licked his lips. God, how I love those lips. I sat up straight, placed my hands on his stomach and rocked my hips back and forth. Mayan smiled and reached in between my legs to play with my aching pearl. I'd never felt a sensation like this.

"Oh," I groaned, barely able to breathe.

Mayan's eyes lustfully narrowed. He was enjoying torturing me. Mr. Mayan Banks knew just how to treat a woman's body and I'm glad he was handling mine the right way.

"Hey, Maria," I acknowledged when I walked in the office Tuesday morning.

"Good afternoon, Mayan," Maria looked over the top of her computer monitor.

Even though my head was buried in my phone, I could feel Maria staring at me. Instead of feeding into it, I continued in my office and sat down at my desk. I had a full schedule and didn't have time to waste.

"Mmhmm," Maria cleared her throat.

I lifted my eyes from the computer screen and saw her leaning against the door frame. Sitting back in my seat with my hands over my head, I waited for her to say what was on her mind. She looked like she was trying to figure out my mood.

"What's on your mind, Maria?"

"Well, since you asked," she walked in with the iPad in her hand. "Is it true you're dating Amor Dames?"

"What makes you ask that?"

It was only a matter of time before Maria questioned it. My phone had been ringing off the hook for the past three days between my mama, my little sisters, Calvin, and even Mo. Everybody wanted to be the first to find out what I was up to and if Amor and I were going public. Honestly, I couldn't answer the question. It's only been three fuckin' days. I don't know what we were. For now, until we talk about it, we're just having sex. A lot of fuckin' sex. Good sex at that.

Maria snapped her fingers in my face to get my attention. I

focused on the screen and then the bold black words. *The Tea with Diane Rose* Instagram page had a new video post. Diane Rose was the bane of my existence. Ever since the world found out I was single; she's been trying to find out who occupies my bed at night. She made it her mission to harass any woman that may have had contact with me. Maria pressed play and I watched the video closely.

"Could it be? Chicago's most eligible bachelor, Mayan Banks, spotted leaving the grand opening of *Mahogany and Crème Nightclub,* with a woman! Reports have named the mystery woman as none other than newly divorced Amor Dames. If you don't know, girl let me tell you. Amor was previously married to football superstar Damon Dames. The ink on their divorce hasn't even dried yet and she's managed to snag another baller. Ms. Amor, if you're watching, let me be the first to say, I'll pay top dollar to hear you teach a class on *Snagging a Rich Man 101.* Whew, chile. Sis is doing it right!"

Pictures of Amor and I exiting the club with my jacket covering her popped up on the screen. *That dress!* Thinking about the treasure of Amor's body, underneath the fabric caused my dick to push against my slacks.

Diane continued her rant and when the picture disappeared, I'd lost interest. There wasn't anything else for me to hear. I stopped the video and took the iPad out of Maria's hand. She giggled before sitting on the corner of my desk and folding her arms.

"What?" I quizzed.

"You know what," she fired back. "What's going on between you two? Is there something I need to know?"

"Maria, when there's something to know, I promise, you'll be the first to hear it."

"If I had to guess, by the smile plastered on your face, there's a whole lot to talk about already. Have you taken her out on a date or anything? Please don't tell me the only thing you've done is play freeze tag under the sheets."

"Freeze tag?" I questioned.

"Yes, freeze tag. When one of you is *it,* you have to *tag* the other person."

For a minute, Maria stared at me like I was supposed to automatically understand her analogy. We waited for a few minutes before I threw my head back in laughter.

"Took you long enough!" She laughed as well. "Mayan, if you really like her, then set up a date. If not, then you need to explain to her that it's only sex and not lead her on. Leading her on is the worst thing to do."

"I hear you, Maria. Let me think on it." I tried my best not to grin at her, but she was making it hard.

Maria was way too excited about me and my love life with Amor. She was probably on her way to finding the best restaurant in town to make a reservation. There was no way she was going to allow me to skip out on taking Amor on a date.

An hour later, I called Maria into my office.

"Hey, Maria."

"Yes?" She asked a little chipper than she had been earlier.

"If I was going to take Ms. Dames on a date, where would *you* recommend, I take her?"

Maria squealed before running out of my office and quickly returning with the iPad in hand. She pulled up the internet browser to show me she was two steps ahead of me. She'd made reservations at several places, all with a variety of food and unique atmospheres. I was impressed. Maria ran down which places she liked at lightning speed. Even though I had picked one already, I allowed her to continue with her presentation. I appreciated how hard she worked on making this special.

As if she read my mind, she stopped talking and looked at me.

"Do any of these stand out?"

"Actually, yes. I like this one."

"Good choice!" Maria gushed. "That's so romantic. It overlooks the river and gives you a beautiful view of the city."

"Great, what day is our reservation."

"Tonight, at eight. Don't be late. I'm going to make sure you're out of here no later than five."

"Seriously?" I laughed. "How'd you know I'd be able to make it tonight?"

"I run your schedule. You aren't missing out on this. You're going to give Ms. Amor, a night to remember. One more thing, I took the liberty of ordering a flower arrangement and having it delivered to her residence. It should be there shortly. You're welcome."

"What would I do without you," I asked, shaking my head.

"I don't know, but let's hope we don't have to find out. I'm going to get back to work. Let me know if you need anything else," Maria called out before walking out and returning to her desk.

Getting through the rest of this day was going to be hard. All I could think about was spending time with Amor. It had been so long since I went on a real date. This should be interesting.

Amor

Mmmm…

With my eyes still closed, I rolled over and buried my face in the pillow Mayan had occupied the prior night. His cologne has saturated the fabric, and I happily welcomed it. A little tingle ran through me as I thought about how he said *see you later* this morning, with his head between my legs. I clenched my thighs together and sucked in a deep breath. Mayan knew how to make a woman feel alive again.

Normally, I'd be tired and ready to stay in bed all day after a night of sex. Not this time though. I was ready to get my day started. Mayan had a bit of caffeine in his dick because I was energized and ready to go! I flipped the comforter off my body and placed my feet on the plush carpet. I stretched and attempted to walk to my bathroom, but every inch of me ached. My legs were gapped as if I had been riding a horse all night.

Moments later, I welcomed the hot water on my skin. Soft R&B music played over the speaker system. I couldn't explain the butterflies I felt as Anita Baker sang about *Sweet Love.* Even though we hadn't put a title on anything, I could get used to having Mayan around all the time. Waking up to those bushy eyebrows, smooth chocolate skin, and thousand-watt smile. Yeah, he had my head in the clouds. I know I shouldn't be thinking about the future this fast, but it was hard not to. *He's* damn near perfect.

Calm down, Amor.

After a deep breath, I shook off thoughts of the future and finished washing my body. Once I was dry and moisturized, I headed down to my kitchen to brew a cup of coffee. An old Toni

Braxton song played as I made my way around the kitchen.

Just as I was in a groove, my doorbell chimed. I picked up my phone and activated my doorbell app. To my surprise, it was Mahogany.

"You have a key!" I yelled into my phone.

"I was being polite hoe! I didn't want to walk in on anything that would make me want to douse my eyes in bleach!" She shot back.

"Whatever, use your key. I'm in the kitchen."

It didn't take Mo long to get in the house and come to the kitchen. I was happy because she had a white plastic bag with two to-go containers. My stomach rumbled at the smell of strawberry Belgium waffles, chicken sausage, and eggs. She placed the bags on the counter and began unpackaging everything.

"So, where's lover boy?" She asked.

"Who?"

"Amor, you know who! Where's Mayan? The way you've been duckin' me the past few days, I figured he'd be over here blowing your back out."

I bit back a smile as I poured a cup of coffee.

"If you must know, he had to go to work. He left early this morning," I placed the cup of coffee to my lips to hide my smile.

"Bitch, you're dick drunk. I can see it all on your face."

"What?" I yelled.

"You heard me. I can see it all on your face. Mayan made you touch the sky, and your ass hasn't come down yet."

"Is it that obvious?" I tried to keep a straight face, but I couldn't help it. My cheeks burned from smiling so much.

"Yes, it's obvious. You got it bad girl."

"Maybe," I responded.

"Maybe?" She questioned. "You can deny it all you want, but your face tells the whole truth and nothing but the truth. I'm happy for you, friend. Glad my grand opening was able to bring you two together. You deserve all the happiness you can get. It's been a long time coming."

Immediately, my mind went back to the last few months. I'd been through hell and back with Damon, Justine, and their lawyers. They tried so hard to leave me with nothing, when I was part of the reason Damon even had a career.

"Nope," Mo snapped in my face. "We aren't about to do that. This isn't about your past anymore. You've overcome that obstacle and now you're starting fresh. You deserve all the good, Amor. Trust me."

Before I could say thank you, my doorbell rang again.

"Are you expecting a package?"

"No, I haven't ordered anything in like a week."

Instead of using my phone, I walked to the door with Mo hot on my tail. When I opened it, I was awed by a beautiful arrangement of white and pink roses. I couldn't lie, my heart swelled. It was thoughtful. I was so in my head about the surprise, I didn't hear the delivery man requesting my signature. Mo stepped in front of me and signed before I grabbed the box and walked in the house.

"And who sent these?" Mo asked once we made it back in the kitchen.

"I don't know, I'm trying to find the card."

I located the card and quickly tore it open. Once again, I could feel my cheeks burning from smiling so hard.

Dinner, tonight at eight. See you at seven.

-Mr. Banks

"Well, what does it say?" Mo asked.

"He wants to take me to dinner…tonight!"

"Oh bitch! You need to start getting ready, now!"

"Uh unn, don't do that," I sassed.

"I didn't mean it like *that.* I was simply saying, we have some work to do to get you ready. I'm already messaging Oya to see if she can squeeze you in for an emergency hair appointment. Oh, what are you going to wear? A dress? What color? Heels? Of course, you're wearing heels," Mo continued having a conversation with herself, while I smelled the roses.

After Mo convinced Oya to squeeze me in, I raced upstairs to get dressed. I hadn't checked my phone since she arrived, and I wasn't surprised at all to find a text from Mayan.

MAYAN: *Can't wait to see you tonight.*

--

"How do I look?" I asked Mo as I twirled.

"Good enough to fuck. Mayan's a very lucky man, Ms. Amor."

"Yeah, he really is," I agreed, trying to hold back a fit of giggles.

"Enjoy yourself tonight, Amor. Don't think too hard about it. It's just a date. Nothing more. Let loose and allow Mayan to treat you the way you deserve to be treated. I love you girl."

Mo kissed me goodbye before heading home for the night and leaving me alone with my thoughts. I prayed I didn't do my usual overthinking.

"Relax, Amor. You've been on plenty of first dates before," I coached, while looking at myself in the floor length mirror.

At seven on the dot, my doorbell chimed.

Punctual.

Taking a deep breath, I reached for the knob and opened it.

There he stood, a 6'4 glass of chocolate milk draped in Tom Ford.

"Wow," Mayan finally spoke. "You look breath taking."

"Thank you," I chuckled like a schoolgirl."

Mayan continued to undress me with his eyes before pulling his hand from behind his back, presenting me with another bouquet of white and pink roses.

"God, these are beautiful."

I placed the roses to my nose and inhaled the scent.

"Just like you."

"Care to come inside while I put these in water?"

"No," he responded.

His bluntness caught me off guard, but I chose not to press the issue before turning around and walking away. Wanting to get back to Mayan, I angrily stuffed the roses in a vase filled with cold water and vowed to tend to them later.

When I returned, Mayan was leaned against his car with his hands clasped in front of him. With attitude to spare, I sauntered over and waited for him to open the door.

"Talk to me, Amor," he requested.

How was I supposed to tell him his decline of my invitation hurt my feelings?

"Why didn't you want to come in?" I finally spoke up.

"You're mad about that?"

"Yes."

"No need to be, love. It was for your own good."

"My own good?" I repeated.

"Yes."

"How so?"

Mayan pushed himself off the car and got in my space. His

eyes stayed on me while he wrapped an arm around my waist and pulled me into his body. Specifically, his rock-hard dick.

"If I went in, we wouldn't have made it to dinner. *You* would be dinner, mi Amor." I tried holding my composure.

Mayan placed his head in the crook of my neck, and we inhaled at the same time.

"Mayan," I begged.

"Hmm?"

"We have to go."

It was a struggle to talk because his hand caressing my thigh was doing serious damage to my mind as well as my panties.

"If you act right tonight, maybe I'll allow you access to what you crave the most. Before we can get there, you must feed me, baby."

"Deal."

Mayan stood up straight and looked at me, I quickly got lost in those perfect brown eyes. I didn't want to look away, however, he did the deed for me. He stepped around me and pulled open the car door.

Once Mayan secured me in the car, he headed out of my driveway. Soft R&B music crooned from his car speakers, setting the perfect mood. No words needed to be spoken. Our bodies spoke the words in our hearts. This was magical.

Occasionally, Mayan would glance over to see if I was okay. It was cool because I was watching him, too. The way his veins stuck out as he gripped the steering wheel and maneuvered through the street was a love language. I damn near melted in my seat when he turned a corner. Knowing that I was watching him closely, Mayan grabbed my hand and brought it to his lips and kissed the back causing goosebumps to appear on my arm. Soon after, he placed his hand on my exposed thigh and kept it there until we made it to the restaurant.

Like a true gentleman, Mayan help me out of the car and held my hand to help ease my nerves. The last time I was public with a man it was Damon. The thought alone made me tense. Mayan noticed and rubbed the back of my hand with his thumb, reassuring me everything would be okay.

When we walked in the building, Mayan led me to the elevator. We were instructed to ride to the top floor where the hostess would greet us. The moment the elevator doors closed, Mayan turned towards me and backed me up against the wall as his chest heaved up and down. My body weakened when he slid his tongue back and forth on his bottom lip. A devious smile crept up on my face in anticipation of what was going to happen next. Mayan wrapped his hand around my neck, applying light pressure, while the other held a vice grip on my thigh.

"What are you doing?" I challenged.

He didn't respond. Instead, his hand inched up my loose fitted skirt until he reached my aching pussy.

"Mayan, someone can get on at any moment," I pleaded breathlessly.

Mayan's fingers separated my folds and began circling my clit. I grabbed a hold of his back and closed my eyes tightly. Mayan continued his assault until I creamed on his fingers…in record time. He eased out of me and proceeded to put his fingers in his mouth just as the door dinged.

"Thanks for my dinner," he boasted.

"I should kill you," I whispered.

My cheeks were visibly flushed from all the excitement. I was sure everyone would notice.

"Go to the bathroom and take those panties off," he whispered in my ear as we stepped out. "I want to keep them as a souvenir."

Mayan pointed in the direction of the bathroom, and I ran off to gather myself.

When Amor returned to the table, she sat across from me and stared me down. I laughed while placing my glass of whiskey to my mouth.

"You're wrong for that. This skirt is light. What would I have done if I got it wet? You want me to sit at dinner with a big ass wet spot on my skirt?"

"Who would have seen it?"

"What?" Amor questioned.

"Who would have noticed?"

"The people in the restaurant, Mayan. That's who."

I raised an eyebrow. She had yet to notice.

"Look around, Amor. No one would have noticed because it's just us."

Amor quickly spun her head around to see we were the only occupants of the restaurant. Maria was aware how I liked to keep things private and went above and beyond to make sure we had the place to ourselves. If I was going to do right by Amor, I was going to give her the world.

"Mayan" she whined. "You didn't have to do that."

"I know. I simply wanted to enjoy this night. It's all about you, mi Amor."

Amor tried to hide the smile on her face by placing the glass of wine to her lips.

"Thank you, Mayan. This is already the best date I've ever been on. This view is breath taking," she complimented while looking out the floor length windows.

It was important to me that Amor enjoyed our evening. Sex wasn't the only thing on my mind, however, seeing her in that dress was making it very hard for me to focus. I knew how to please a woman four ways to Sunday with sex. It was natural for me. But I wanted to give Amor more than just sex. Although I wasn't going to turn down the opportunity to get between those thick ass thighs.

It gripped my heart to watch Amor talk to the server with class and grace, as she ordered what she wanted off the menu. She embodied more sex appeal than I'd ever seen in my thirty-two years of living. Her hair was freshly done in a huge donut-like bun on top of her head revealing all her facial features. She was worth every fuckin' dime I spent to rent this place. A rare gem.

Once our food arrived, Amor loosened up. We ate, laughed, shared intimate details about our lives and our hopes for the future. Amor even went as far as telling me about her heartbreak with Damon. She'd basically helped Damon become the superstar he is today. She did everything but score the damn touchdowns herself. Amor helped him train, kept him fed, found him a worthy agent, assisted in contract negotiations yet mindfully be the *woman* he needed. When he had no one else, he had her. She saw potential in him when no one else did. She built *the* man, but in the end, he left her for another woman.

Amor was different. She didn't harbor resentment or ill feelings towards Damon, and I applauded her. The more we talked, the more I realized how badly I wanted this woman. I can't lie and say I wasn't worried about being the man *she* needed. My previous relationship complicated things for me.

"What happened during your last relationship," Amor quizzed. "I can't be the only one sharing my deepest darkest thoughts."

Last thing I wanted to talk about was my relationship with Zara, while I envisioned bending Amor over. As much as I care about her, I felt it was necessary to be open. I placed the glass of whiskey to my lips and took a healthy gulp. I was going to need it to get through this conversation.

"Her name is Zara Stevens."

"The super model?"

I could see the panic in Amor's eyes.

"Yes."

Silence.

"We dated during the time we were at the peak of our careers. She landed a seven-figure contract, and I was one of the best running backs in the league. Everybody thought I was going to help lead my team to the Super Bowl."

"I remember," she spoke softly with a twinge of sadness. "Instead, you blew your knee out against Buffalo during *Week Twelve.*"

"Yeah."

A sharp pain ripped through my knee. I discreetly rubbed it under the table.

"Surgery, rehab, and therapy were a lot for me to deal with. I wasn't the nicest person to be around. I was only focused on making a comeback. My relationship was the last thing on my mind, and I allowed Zara to slip through my fingers. She found a nigga to give her the consistency she was looking for. I would have appreciated her at least coming to tell me she was done, but I had to find out from the blogs and pictures of her leaving hotel rooms with Marquis Moore."

"Your own teammate?"

"Yeah."

"I'm sorry about that."

"It's all good. Since then, I haven't done the relationship thing," I admitted.

"Why?"

"Wasn't sure, I was able to give a woman what she was looking for. I've been focused on my businesses and feeding my family. A lot of people depend on me to make shit happen."

The more I talked, the more I could see the glimmer of hope in her eyes disappearing.

"What about your happiness? Doesn't that matter?"

"I'm happy seeing the people I love taken care of, not worrying about anything."

"Oh."

Amor was staring at me, but her gaze was very distant. She was overthinking.

"Amor," I called out her name.

She slightly shook her head and blinked a few times.

"Mi Amor, get out of your head," I demanded.

"I'm fine," she lied, with a fake smile.

"Come here."

"What?"

"Don't make me repeat myself."

Amor looked around to see if any of the wait staff was watching. I didn't give a fuck if they were. I knew where her head was, and I needed to ease the uncertainty. The person I was *then* isn't who I am *now.*

"Amor!"

Hearing how serious I was, Amor removed the napkin from her lap and placed it on the table before walking to me. She timidly stood in front of me, trying to figure out my next move.

"What, Mayan? Why did I need to come over here?"

I turned towards her and pulled her between my legs. I had the best view of her breasts. She looked down at me after feeling the heat of my breath on her skin. If I didn't say what was on my mind, I would end up devouring her.

"Amor, everything I said was past tense. I never thought I'd be able to give a woman a relationship and all that comes with it... until I met you. When I laid eyes on you, I knew this was it. It's been less than a week and I'm ready to take you home to meet my mama. I can barely focus on my work. When I'm with you, you consume me. Everything about you makes me fall deeper and deeper for you. I find myself wanting to give you everything you've ever dreamed of."

Amor inhaled slowly and closed her eyes, while I rubbed on her silky thighs.

"Tell me how I can ease your doubt."

"I don't doubt you Mayan."

"Yes, you do."

I didn't give Amor a chance to say anything else, I slipped a finger in the open area of her shirt and toyed with her protruding nipple. When I went to put my hand in, she grabbed a hold of my wrist.

"We're in public."

"I don't give a fuck."

"But I do. There are eyes and cameras everywhere, Mayan. Do you want pictures of us fuckin' in a restaurant to be plastered over the internet? I sure as hell don't."

"Amor. Look at this," I stated, nodding to the bulge in my pants. "You gonna turn him down?"

"If you hurry up and get us out of here, maybe we can take care of it in my house or yours."

"Shit, as you wish mi Amor."

Mayan stood from his seat and adjusted the middle of his pants. He had a devious look on his face before he took his finger and lifted my chin. He gave me an intense and passionate kiss. I let out a low moan as I tried to catch my breath. He pressed his hard dick on my thigh. I reached down and started to stroke it, to tease him. His body shuttered against mine. He cocked his head to the side as a warning to stop playing with fire.

"Let's go," he instructed. "I'm 'bout to fuck the shit outta you."

He barely gave me time to grab my things before he whisked me off my feet and walked towards the elevator. I smiled as I kicked my legs in the air joyfully. I wrapped my arms around his shoulders before placing my fingers on top of his head and massaging his waves.

"I want to know everything there is to know about you, Mayan Banks. The good, the bad, and the ugly."

"Are you sure you want that? The ugly can get really ugly."

"I'm sure and in return, I'll let you know some things about me."

"Some? It sounds like you're trying to keep some things from me. Is that what you're trying to do?" Mayan followed up his question by smacking my ass.

I squinted my eyes and hissed at him. My ass was stinging from that love tap. As soon as the elevator doors opened, flashes from cameras blinded us to the point I had to shield my eyes.

"How did they know we were here?" I yelled in Mayan's ear,

trying to shield them from seeing my lust filled face. The reporters fired off question after question.

"Somebody in the building probably tipped them off."

Hesitantly, Mayan placed me on my feet once we were out of the elevator. He held out his hand and I placed mine in his. A surge of electricity flowed through our bodies and caused us to gaze intensely at one another. The camera's continued to flash as we made it to his car.

"Amor!" A woman's voice called out and I looked back. "Girl, give us the tea! The ladies and I want to know…is he as good as the rumors say he is?"

That damn Diane Rose. I saw her little post on Instagram telling me to teach a class about snagging a baller. Bitch lost her funky ass mind. I chuckled her way before dipping my head in the passenger seat of Mayan's car. He closed the door, He quickly got in and pulled off before they could ask me more questions.

"Messy bitch. They always seem to find us."

"It's cool. I don't have anything to hide when it comes to you. Diane can dig around all she wants."

"I like the way you're talking."

"Only for you, mi Amor."

"I love when you call me that," I spoke seductively. "Makes me feel some kind of way."

By now, the expensive wine I'd consumed had traveled right to my pussy. I wanted now more than ever to hop on top of that long thick pole and ride the waves of ecstasy.

"How does it make you feel?"

Mayan inched his hand up my thigh and I quickly slapped it away. He was always taking care of *me*. It was now my turn to take care of him. I reached over and began undoing his belt buckle. Mayan got comfortable in his seat and allowed me to unzip his pants and run my fingers along the top seam of his boxers. The closer I inched to the head of his dick, the more my heart raced. I couldn't wait to feel his grith stretching my mouth.

He pulled in a sharp breath as my lips touched the head of his dick. I savored the salty taste of the pre-cum oozing from the tip. I'd never seen a dick this pretty. He was damn near perfect, and it was all mine. I took as much of him as I could into my mouth and went to work. I smiled slyly as Mayan shifted and groaned in his seat.

"Damn, baby."

He grabbed the back of my neck and gave it a firm squeeze. I continued to bob my head up and down mercilessly. The moment I felt him swelling within my mouth, I sped up the pace and wrapped both my hands around it. I'd done a pretty good job of making him believe I was this timid woman who could receive pleasure, but not deliver. The combination of my hands twisting around his shaft and the tightness of my mouth had him going crazy.

"Amor, fuck!" Mayan growled.

"Eyes on the road. Focus on not crashing this car," I spoke up, not missing one damn beat.

Mayan rotated his hips and quickly pumped in and out of my mouth.

"Shit, here I come Amor. Swallow all that shit," he demanded while erupting in my throat. "Fuck! Damn girl, you gonna make me marry your ass."

I finished cleaning him off and slid his semi hard dick back into his pants. When I sat up, Mayan had a smirk on his face. If I knew better, our night was far from over. We were just getting started.

"You know, paybacks a bitch, right?"

"I look forward to it."

--

Mayan entered the gates of his home and drove up the long driveway. He quickly placed the car in park and hopped out. I went to grab my purse and phone but stopped when my door was yanked open. I spun around to see Mayan with a demonic look in his eyes. He grabbed a hold of my ankle and turned me around in my seat. Not wasting any time, he got down on the ground, fuck the nice pants he was wearing, and ripped my skirt in half. I was completely exposed. He didn't give me much time to dwell on it. The first touch of his tongue on my pearl made me gasp.

"Mayan! Wait, can we make it inside the house?" I yelped.

"Nah, you didn't wait until we made it inside. So, neither will I," he shrugged like it was that simple. "Sit back and shut the fuck up while I eat this shit."

"Okay!" I screamed while clawing at his head.

Mayan was torturing me. I couldn't stay still to save my life. I kicked my legs and pulled at my hair. I never knew such bliss existed.

"You like that shit, Amor?"

"Yes!" I yelled as I moved my hips to match the rhythm of his tongue.

"I don't think you do. I think this is bad. Am I doing a terrible job?"

"Shut up talking! I'm about to cum!"

As if I said the magic word, Mayan went full force. Clinging onto the back of the seat I lost all control of my body. I was the puppet, and he was the master. I climaxed in a matter of seconds.

Mayan got off the ground with his beard glistening with my juices. I reached forward, grabbed his shirt, and kissed him passionately.

"I'm not done," he growled in my mouth.

Mayan picked me up out of the car and I wrapped my legs around his waist. He carried me up the front steps and into the house. I gave him hot kisses on his face and neck, before licking and sucking on his ear.

When we made it to his bedroom, he tossed me on the bed, and I ripped his shirt open. Not giving a damn about the buttons. His chocolate skin glistened under the glare of the moonlight coming through his floor-to-ceiling windows.

"You like what you see?" He questioned, knowing damn well the answer was yes.

I nodded and smiled.

"Use your words Amor," he probed, massaging in between my folds. "Do you like what you see?"

"Yes, Mr. Banks" I let out breathlessly.

"I like that shit," he acknowledged. "Turn over for me."

Doing as I was told, I turned over and got on all fours and showed off my deep arch. He grabbed me by my ankles and yanked me to the edge of the bed. I guess we were saying fuck the soft sensual shit.

"Damn," he mumbled.

Mayan placed the tip of his dick at my opening and rubbed it up and down, lubricating the area. Without warning, he pushed himself inside of me. I grabbed a hold of the sheets and gasped as he stretched me wide.

"Fuck," he moaned lowly.

The soft sensual strokes he delivered to my body sent me into another dimension. He pressed his chest against my back and placed soft kisses on my spine along with firm hits to my ass.

"Baby," I cried out. "I can't take it anymore.

I tried to reach back and place my hand on his chest to stop him. He quickly swatted it away.

"Be a good girl, Amor and take this dick. Don't tap out on me."

"I can't. I can't!"

"Yes, you can," he coached. "Damn, this pussy looks so fuckin' good grippin' this dick. This shit so fuckin' pretty, Amor."

Mayan was losing control. He delivered five forceful blows to my ass before digging his hands on either side of my hips. Sweat trickled from my body and his as he sped up his thrusts.

"I'm about to cum!" I yelled.

"That's right, Amor. Nut on this dick."

I clawed, screamed, and bit down on the sheets trying to control myself, but there was no use. He was fucking away all my logic and reasoning.

"Yess!!!" I screamed as the walls of my pussy clenched down on his dick.

"That's right. Make a mess for me, Amor."

I'd lost feeling in my body and collapsed on the bed. Two tears fell from my eyes as I hugged the sheets. What we just did should have been a fuckin' sin…

Amor lay next to me, breathing softly as her small fingers trailed across my chest. As much as I loved being in her soft pink matter, I decided to leave her be after seeing her limp to the bathroom. For now, we were enjoying listening to our synchronized hearts beat. A few candles illuminated the space casting a soft glow on her face.

"You know we go together, right?" Amor spoke up.

"Oh, word?"

"Hell yeah. You've put your mouth on me several times and gave me the best dick I've ever had in life. Ain't no way I'm letting another bitch get that."

"Territorial. I like that," I let out a hearty laugh.

"As long as you know. You're *mine* Mayan Banks."

"I'm with it, Amor Daniels. I'm all yours."

Amor's head shot up at the sound of me calling her by her maiden name. I'm sure she thought I didn't know. I figured she would want to detach herself from Damon, sooner or later. There was no better time to start than with her getting her name back.

"How'd you know about that?"

"I do my homework. Is that cool with you?"

"Actually," she took a long pause. "It's been so long since I've heard *my* last name. But to answer your question, yes. It's perfectly fine."

"Good, because now that we *go together*, I ain't callin' you by that nigga's last name."

"Now who's being territorial?"

"Whatever, I meant what I said."

"I hear you, baby," she spoke softly before placing her hand on my cheek and getting closer to me.

"I got you, Amor."

I placed my arm around her waist and leaned forward to place a kiss on her forehead. As much as it scared me to be in another committed relationship, something about this woman made me want to give her the world. And just like that, light snores came from her mouth.

--

The clattering of pots and pans woke me up. Checking my clock, it was well before eight in the morning. I'd purposely told Maria I wouldn't be in the office today because I planned on sleeping in. Amor lay with her mouth slightly ajar, not fazed by the noise coming from the kitchen.

Inching out of the bed, I threw on some sweats and a t-shirt before walking down the stairs to see who'd invaded my space. The smell of pancakes and bacon hit my nose and made my stomach to rumble. Even though the food smelled amazing, and it was needed, I gotta tell my mama there was no poppin' up and doing this shit anymore. Especially since Amor and I only made things official last night.

When I made it to the kitchen, she had her back to me, humming gospel music and mixing batter. I leaned against the island, folded my arms, and cleared my throat. She turned around with a smile on her face.

"Hey mama's baby. I called the office to see if you'd be in today and Maria told me you'd taken a personal day. I figured I'd come over and surprise you with some food."

I walked over to where she was and kissed her forehead.

"Did Maria say anything else?" I probed.

"Maybe."

"Maybe? That's a yes. What else did she say?"

"Oh nothing, the usual."

"Ma, don't lie for her."

"Ugh," she rolled her eyes and put her hands on her hip. "Maria told me you and Amor went on your first date last night. I wanted to hear how it went so I figured I come over, we have a wonderful breakfast, and you tell me all about it."

"That would be good and all if she wasn't still here."

My mom clasped her hands together and shook her head.

"I'm so sorry! Let me finish up here and get out of your way. I didn't know y'all had reached the *sleepover phase.*"

"I'm sure it's fine, ma. Let me go wake her up and see."

"I don't think you need to," she spoke as she looked past me.

Turning on my heels, I saw Amor dressed in one of my longer t-shirts and a pair of boxers. Her thick, honey-colored legs were on display as she bashfully played with her fingernails. She looked so fuckin' good. The sweet and innocent vibes she was giving off had my mind blown.

"Hi," she said shyly. "I felt the bed shift and wanted to see if everything was okay."

"It's all good. Uh," I scratched the top of my head, unsure of how to make this introduction.

"Don't mind him and his manners. Good morning, Ms. Amor," my mom spoke up. "I'm Nora, Mayan's mother. Excuse me for my intrusion. I didn't know you were still here. I made breakfast if you're hungry. I'm going to go on and get out of here."

"It's okay," Amor chuckled. "I promise. I'd love for you to stay and enjoy this wonderful meal with us."

She's a keeper.

My mom looked at me and I nodded my head in approval.

"We'd love to have you join us."

Fifteen minutes later, Amor and my mother were sitting at the table having a conversation. They didn't even act like I was here. They talked like two longtime friends. Amor was perfect and my mother was eating it up. They'd made plans to have a *girl's day* on my dime that consisted of manicures, pedicures, and massages. As long as they're happy, I don't give a damn. Seeing them get along made me fall for Amor even harder. This was the type of shit I've been waiting on.

"When you come over, I'll have to show you all of Mayan's baby pictures," my mom called out before giving Amor a hug.

"Ma, please. Don't."

"Awww, baby Mayan, I'd love to see it," Amor gushed.

"I got you, honey. He can't keep us apart. You kids go ahead and enjoy the rest of your day. Thank you for allowing me to invade your morning. Mayan, I'll see you soon. Amor—"

"I'll be sure to call you later today to get the pancake recipe."

They shared in a warm embrace before Amor went back in the house and I walked my mom to the car.

"Mayan."

"Ma'am?"

"I like this one. Keep her please."

"I'll try. Get home safe. Let me know when you make it."

I never thought I'd enjoy meeting someone's mother as much as I enjoyed meeting mama Nora. Everything about her was warm and inviting. I've met my fair share of moms and she's by far the best I've encountered. I know all of this is new and fresh, but I don't want to come down from the high.

After kissing his mother goodbye, I allowed them to have a moment to themselves and made my way back into the kitchen to clean. Nora cleaned as she cooked, but our plates and utensils were left behind. Taking care of them was the least I could do. I looked under the sink in search of dish washing liquid. I didn't want to ask Mayan because I knew he would tell me to leave it alone. My parents raised me better so I was just going to do it before he could protest.

"Clorox…409…where's the damn dish soap? Ah, there it is."

Before I could stand up, I felt a pair of hands on my waist and a hard dick pressed against my ass cheeks.

"Mayan," I moaned as he rubbed my thighs. "What are you doing?"

"Trying to see how this pussy feels in the morning."

"Just like it does at night," I giggled as I tried to wiggle my way out of his grasp. "If you'll excuse me, I have dishes to wash."

"I have a housekeeper," he responded.

"I understand, however, I'm right here and fully capable of cleaning the few dishes left. Now back up and let me work."

Mayan huffed before stepping back and allowing me to start the dishes. He sat at the kitchen island and pouted like a little kid.

"Don't pout, I'll be done soon."

"Whateva."

"Your mom is the most adorable woman I've ever met. So chill and down to earth."

"Uh huh," Mayan responded.

"Mayan Banks," I called out his name with my hands on my hips. "If you're going to sit there and pout this entire time, go upstairs or something."

"You tryna tell me what to do now?"

I gave him a stern look and shrugged my shoulders. Mayan smiled, before toying with the hairs on his chin. He jumped up from his chair, raced around the counter and picked me up.

"Put me down," I kicked my feet in a fit of laughter.

"Okay, bet."

Mayan put me down on the counter and began lifting up the bottom of my shirt while placing kisses on my neck.

"W-what are you doing?"

"I can't seem to get enough of you."

I sighed, giving in to his affection. I can't seem to get enough of him either.

"You like when I do this to you?"

Mayan pushed past the fabric of the boxers and made his way to my clit.

"Yesss," I hissed.

My body started shaking and my heart started to beat uncontrollably. No matter what he did, he always knew how to make feel so damn good. I inhaled and exhaled slowly as he gripped my face with his massive hand and pushed it to the side, allowing him full access to my neck. He trailed his tongue from my collarbone, up to my jawline before stopping at my lips. He sucked my bottom lip between his teeth and bit down lightly before letting a moan escape his lips. I reached down between my legs and stroked his erection through his pants.

"Pull it out," he demanded.

I complied.

Mayan rubbed his fingers up and down the spine of my back.

"Spread those legs."

I spread my legs as far as they could go, showing off my flexibility. Mayan looked down, licked his lips, and nodded his head in approval. He eased a finger inside of me causing my back to arch.

"Mayan!" I screamed out.

"Yeah, you like this shit."

"Yes!" I moaned.

My body tensed as an orgasm ripped through me. I grabbed a hold of him, dug my fingers into his back, and bit down on his shoulder.

"Shit," I whimpered.

Mayan didn't give me a chance to breathe before taking the tip of his dick and shoving it into my opening. He heatedly pumped in and out of me. The sound of our body's attempting to fuse together and our heavy breathing echoed off the walls.

"You're so fuckin' beautiful, Amor Daniels."

"I lo—" I had to stop myself before I finished the sentence.

Mayan leaned his head back to see my entire face, making sure to not miss a beat. He caught wind of what I was going to say and gave me a smirk. He picked up the pace sending me into a frenzy as I clawed at his back. The pain didn't bother him. He took it like a muthafuckin' champ.

"Get this nut, Amor."

I contracted my pussy walls to milk him dry.

"Fuck," he growled. "I love this shit, Amor. Don't fuckin' stop."

He closed his eyes as he released inside of me. He rested his head on my shoulder as we caught our breath.

"Damn," he grumbled as he pulled out of me.

My legs felt like mush, so he walked me to the bedroom.

This is fuckin' magical.

Mayan

It was around one in the afternoon. Amor and I were laid up talking. We were both naked, enjoying each other's company. Her thick legs were intertwined with mine and her head rested on my chest.

"As much as I wanna lay in bed all day between these thick ass thighs, I think it's best we get out the house. Anything on your mind that you want to do?"

Amor placed her hand under her chin and thought about it.

"Actually," she smiled. "I'd love to take you somewhere. Are you up for a little adventure?"

"I'm all yours today. Whatever you want, you can have it."

Amor's smile touched the corners of her eyes as she kissed my lips.

"I don't have anything to wear though."

"It's taken care of. I'll be back."

Hopping out the bed, I went downstairs to grab the bag Mo put together and Calvin dropped off.

"Here, Mo put this together for you."

I dropped the heavy ass duffle bag on the floor next to the bed. Amor jumped up naked, breast bouncing, in excitement.

"Aww, best friend knows me well."

"What the fuck you got in that heavy ass bag."

"All the necessities. Now if you'll excuse me, I'm gonna go freshen up."

Amor's naked ass switched towards the bathroom. The sway of her ass caused my dick to spring to life. I couldn't get enough.

"I'm comin' with you."

She turned on her heels fast as hell and placed her hand on my chest.

"No sir! If you follow me into that shower, we're fuckin' *again* and we don't want that."

"You gone leave him hard like this?"

We both looked down.

"Yup!" Amor walked to the bathroom, slammed the door, and locked it.

--

An hour and a half later, I was dressed and waiting for Amor to come downstairs. She was pissed I fucked up her hair. She said it was going to take a miracle or some shit to get it decent looking again. After five more minutes, she came walking down the stairs. Her hair was in a slicked back ponytail at the back of her head. She was wearing olive green leggings that looked like they had been painted on her skin, a tan-colored sports bra, and short jacket to match the pants.

"You look good."

"Thank you, you don't look too bad yourself. Now let's go!"

Amor pecked my lips before walking towards the garage. Before I could grab my car keys, Amor jumped in front of me and snatched them off the wall.

"Fuck no!"

"You don't know where we're goin. It's a surprise so obviously, I have to drive. I'm a stellar driver so there's nothing for you to worry about. Let's go."

"Amor," I groaned. "I don't let just anybody drive my shit."

"So, I'm *nobody?*" She asked, while stepping in my space and looking up at me.

Those beautiful ass eyes, man. They got me every fuckin' time.

"Don't fuck up my shit."

"Yeah whatever, nigga. Come on."

Amor popped the locks on my Jeep and jumped in the driver's seat. Being in the passenger seat was a foreign concept. I gripped the side door as Amor backed out of the garage and into the driveway.

So far, so good.

"Mayan, breathe. I'm serious, I know how to drive."

Amor made it out of the gate and onto the main road. I sat back in the seat and did as she said. She turned on some R&B shit and my body tensed. During the day, I listened to straight Hip-Hop. This was going to take some time to get used to. Her ass was singing and dancing the whole way there.

Twenty minutes, later, Amor pulled into the parking lot of an older building. Amor was quiet on where we were, and I decided to go with the flow. She grabbed a hold of my hand and pulled me to the rusted door. From the outside, you would have thought this place was abandoned and rundown. Inside was a clean and nice sized dance studio.

"Mayan, get ready to meet my kids," she whispered.

Kids? When the fuck? Did she have kids?

"Hey my babies!" Amor yelled when she walked into the building.

"Amor!" A big ass group of girls ranging from ages six to about thirteen charged towards Amor and hugged her tight.

"We missed you Ms. Amor. Where have you been?" One girl asked with her hands on her hips.

"Ms. Amor who's that?" Another asked pointing at me.

"Calm down y'all. I know you have a lot of questions and I'm gonna try to answer them all. Sorry I've been away but y'all know how my schedule gets. But I'm here now and I have a lot of free time now, so I can come by more often."

"Yay!"

"Let me stop being rude though," Amor spoke up walking towards me. "This is my friend Mayan."

Friend? Friends don't fuck like we do.

"Hi Mayan!" The girls screamed.

"Hey ladies, it's nice to meet you all."

"Amor you haven't danced with us in *forever.* Can you do a routine with us?"

"Girl, I don't think I can get down like that anymore."

The girls collectively started egging Amor on until she finally gave in. I took a seat in one of the metal chairs on the side and watched as Amor and the girls stretched.

"Show us what you got Ms. A!"

Up tempo music started playing from a speaker and Amor closed her eyes and rotated her head. She allowed the beat of the music to penetrate her body and moved with ease. Every eye in the room was on her as she moved effortlessly to the beat. Amor and the music had become one. By the time she was done, she opened her eyes and asked the girls to join her. They mimicked her moves and were having the time of their lives. When the song ended, I stood up and clapped my hands.

"Aye, that was dope as hell."

"Care to join us?" Amor yelled out.

"Nah, I'm gonna leave the dancing to the professionals. I'll run the music if necessary."

"Thanks for having me girls. I do miss y'all and I'm going to make sure to stop by more often."

I hugged all of my babies before grabbing my purse and walking over to Mayan. The gleam in his eye told me all I needed to know. He enjoyed seeing this part of me and it felt so damn good.

"Hey Amor," Stacy, the team's director called out. "Got a minute to talk?"

"Of course."

"Baby, I'll meet you in the car," Mayan spoke up before kissing my cheek and walking away.

As soon as Mayan walked away, Stacy grabbed my arm and shook it.

"Amor, he's so cute. I'm so damn happy for you."

"Thank you, girl," I gushed. "He truly is something else."

"A big step up from Damon," she scoffed and rolled her eyes. "But anyway, I don't know if you know this, but Damon stopped making payments. We have until the end of the week to pay up or leave. It's way too much money for these girls to afford."

"Are you serious?"

"I wish I was lying. The notice was on the door when I came in today."

Boiling with furry, I ground my teeth and clenched my jaw so tight, it hurt. Despite how Damon felt, paying for the studio was a part of our divorce settlement. He knew how much this studio meant to me, as well as the girls in my old neighborhood. I rented this space to help give these girls a safe place to dance and hangout.

"I'm going to get to the bottom of this, Stacy. I swear. Even if I have to drain my bank account, this place isn't going to get shut down."

"I know you will, Amor. If you need any help from me, let me know and I got you."

I hugged Stacy goodbye before getting in Mayan's truck and slamming the door shut.

"Problem?"

"No," I lied.

"Amor," he growled.

"I'm sorry, there's some stuff going on with the building I need to take care of. Nothing I can't handle."

Mayan looked at me, grabbed a hold of my face and pulled it in his direction.

"If there was a problem, would you tell me?"

Expressionless, I nodded my head. Although I should have told him what was happening, I didn't want to bring problems from my last relationship into my current one. I was going to fix this on my own and the first step was contacting Damon to see why the fuck he wasn't paying. Mayan looked at me for a little longer, before kissing my lips and starting up the car. He pulled out of the buildings parking lot and drove through the streets. He turned on some music and I leaned my head against the window and nodded off.

--

Night had fallen by the time Mayan pulled into my driveway. A part of me didn't want to let him go, but I knew he had work to do. One thing I wasn't going to do was keep a man from making money.

"I had fun today. I liked seeing you in your element."

Mayan stood with his hands on the doorframe of the car. He leaned down, placed a kiss on my forehead and smiled.

"It wasn't my element," I blushed. "Just something I do in my free time."

"Doesn't seem like it. The way you moved to the music was magical. If I had to guess, you've been dancing since you were a little girl. Ballet, tap, and a little jazz. Am I right?"

I shied my eyes away from his and focused on a piece of lent on his jeans. I could feel the heat of a blush on my cheeks.

"Guess that's a yes. Why didn't you take it all the way? You clearly have exactly what it takes."

"The direction of my life changed. That's the past. This is the future. I enjoy dancing with the girls for fun."

Mayan's eyes burned into me. He wanted to know more, and it was killing him to not ask me more questions. I guess he could sense my uneasiness and decided to not push the subject.

"When am I going to see you again?" I broke the awkward tension starting to form.

"Tomorrow after work, I'll come over and we'll put our cooking skills to the test."

"I'd like that."

Mayan leaned in again and placed a kiss on my lips. I grabbed ahold of his chin and rubbed his neat, coarse beard.

"Mmm," I moaned in his mouth.

'Stop. You keep this shit up and I'm gonna have to bend your ass over."

"Is that a threat?"

"Don't tease me, Amor. Get your pretty ass in the house."

Mayan helped me out of the car, and like the gentleman he is, walked me up the steps and made sure I was safe and secure before leaving. I placed my back against the door and let out the biggest breath. Everything about Mayan Banks had me on a high and I never wanted to come down.

Mayan

"Sup, nigga?"

Calvin didn't call my phone often. When he did, it was it was to check on me and talk shit. If I had to guess, Mo ran back and told him I asked her to drop clothes off for Amor.

"Shit, you tell me. What's good?"

"You a gossipin' ass nigga now?"

"How you know I'm callin' to gossip?"

"'Cuz, I know Mo ass done told you what I asked her to do."

"Okay, well then elaborate muthafucka. Is this thing serious between you two? What's goin' on? I already know you dickin' her down."

"Mo ass got you checkin' on me to see if I'm gonna fuck her girl over. Trust me I'm not. Amor is a good woman and I ain't tryna fuck it up. Plus, she met my OG already."

"Daaammmmnn, she met mama already? How the fuck that happened?"

"Ma walked her ass in my house tryna cook me breakfast and shit. Didn't know Amor had come back to my place. You know how it goes."

"Trust me nigga, I do."

"Yeah, I fuck with, Amor. I'm gon' treat her right no doubt."

"Aight, nigga. Make sure you do. I like fuckin' my wife every night. You fuck Amor over and nigga I won't be able to sniff the pussy for at least a month. Mo's gonna be callin' my ass everything but a child of God because of *you.* Don't fuck it up nigga."

"I ain't. Nigga, damn. Calm your spastic ass down. It's gonna all work out. She's the first woman I actually want to do right by."

"Whateva, nigga. Here comes Mo loudmouth ass. Holla at you later."

We ended the call and I started shaking my head as I pulled into my garage. This was gonna take some getting used to. It's been so long since I've been in a relationship, I gotta go back in my memory bank to remember what to do and not do.

"Damn, Amor. What the fuck are you doin' to me?"

"Mo, I'm ready to get in the tub. I'm glad you've enjoyed all the juicy details but now my body needs to soak."

"That's what happens when the dick is bomb. Damon wasn't hittin' it that shit right so you ain't know about that after sex soreness."

"Mo!"

"What I do?"

"Girl bye. Yes, the dick is bomb but it's not why I'm sore. Did you not hear me tell you how I was out there dancing for my life with those girls?"

"That's what yo' ass gets for tryna show off for Mayan. But I need to know what you're going to do about the building. Are you going to pay the money or make Damon's ass do the right thing?"

"I'm not sure yet. I want to call him and curse him out, but I also want to protect my peace. I have more than enough money to pay for it, but it's the principle. I did send him a text saying we needed to talk, ASAP. We'll see if he responds."

"Do you really think Damon is going to do *the right thing*? His ass couldn't even be faithful to the woman who made him who he is! The nigga wouldn't have half the shit he has without you. Then he left you for that bitch Justine Whitehall. Prancing around high on life because she's suckin' black—"

"Mo!"

Whenever Mo got started, she didn't stop. She went full throttle and I always had to reel her back in. I think she was more hurt by the divorce than I was.

"My bad. You know how I get behind you. I witnessed the damage he did and if murder was legal…he'd be gone first."

"Mo, I promise, it's all good. Damon is going to get his karma. I'm honestly not worried about it. Now I'm even mad I texted him. Nonetheless, I'm good."

"Alright, Amor. If that nigga says some slick shit, you better tell me. You know I'm ready for whatever. I'll bring out my black Air Force One energy!"

"No, the fuck you won't!" Calvin yelled in the background.

"You know what it is, Amor."

"Yeah, MoMo, I know."

The sound of my doorbell rang throughout my home. Checking the time on my phone, it was well after eleven at night.

"Who the hell is that ringing your doorbell this late at night? Do I need to call Mayan?"

"No, bitch. Let me go see who it is."

I guess I wasn't answering the door fast enough because they kept pressing the button repeatedly.

"I'm fuckin' coming!"

Standing on the tips of my toes, I looked through the peephole and immediately rolled my eyes.

"Damon's here," I whispered in the phone.

"Oh, hell no! I'm about to either call the cops or have Calvin call Mayan. Cal! Cal, call Mayan! That nigga Damon is beating down Amor's door."

"Amor! I know you're in there. Open the door," Damon yelled out.

"What do you want, Damon?"

"You said we needed to talk, I'm here to talk."

"Not like this! You don't show up to somebody's house unannounced. I'll call you when I'm ready to talk."

Damon let out a long breath filled with frustration and disdain.

"Just open the door. Let's get this shit over with."

"Amor, don't you open that fuckin' door," Mo yelled.

"If I don't, he won't go away. I don't think he's stupid enough to try anything. If you don't hear from me in twenty minutes, call the police."

I ended the call with Mo as Damon continued banging on the door. I swung the door open with more force than intended and stared him down. There he was, the six-foot-three, light skinned, bald-headed, pain in my ass, ex-husband.

"You gonna let me in?"

"Hell no!"

I stepped outside and cracked the door behind me. Unsure of what do say or do, I folded my arms across my chest and waited. Damon stood in front of me with his hands stuffed in his pockets pacing back and forth. This was the first time I'd seen him since the judge finalized our divorce and he was sitting across the table from me, with that bitch at his side. Just thinking about it made me want to lay hands on him. Knowing it wouldn't be the right thing to do, I pushed the thought to the back of my mind.

"Why did you stop paying on the building? You know how much that place means to me and those girls."

"Slipped my mind."

"Stop bullshitting, Damon. You know damn well it didn't slip your fuckin' mind. You forget I know you better than that. Even though I was the one physically paying the bills, you made sure I paid them on-time like clockwork. So, it didn't fuckin' slip your mind."

"What if I don't wanna pay it anymore?" He said, emphasizing each word. "Huh? Have you thought about that? What if I want your dreams and aspirations to come crashing down?"

I was too stunned to speak. I took a step back and clutched my chest.

"You're out here parading around town with another nigga. How am I supposed to feel? It ain't been a week and my teammates are clowning me. How am I supposed to live like this? Answer me"

"You aren't supposed to feel shit, nigga! I'm not your woman anymore!"

"What if I fucked up? Have you thought about that? What if I fucked up and wanted to come back home? I can't do that if you got another nigga sniffin' behind your prissy ass!"

"There it is. There it fuckin' is! You're jealous. You can't stand the thought of me being happy with someone else, even though, you did this to us. Let's not forget, *you* cheated on *me.* Not the other way around. You left this marriage to be with Justine muthafuckin' Whitehall! Get the fuck off my porch with this bullshit. Pay the damn building rent or I'm calling my lawyer!"

I turned around to go back in the house, but Damon yanked me back by my arm.

"You fuckin' that nigga, Amor? Look at this little shit you're wearin' right now. You ain't never wore no shit like this for me? Your ass cheeks practically hanging out."

I wasn't wearing anything out of the ordinary. I had on a pair of workout shorts and an old cut off LSU t-shirt.

"Unhand me, bitch!"

"Does he fuck you better than me?"

I looked off in the distance as I quickly reminisced about the many positions Mayan had put me in the night before. I guess me taking time to think about it pissed Damon off even more. He hemmed me up against the door with his chest heaving up and down. His eyes squeezed into thin slits.

"Let me go, Damon! You're fuckin' crazy!"

"Is there a muthafuckin' problem we need to address?"

Damon and I focused our attention on the voice in the distance.

The only thought in my mind was how I was gonna lay this bitch ass nigga out. Cal called me back to tell me Amor's ex-husband decided to do a surprise pop up. I knew how unpredictable niggas could be and I wasn't taking any fuckin' chances. I stopped everything I was doing and broke all the traffic laws to get to her. If the nigga breathed on her wrong, I was going to knock his ass out.

"Let her go."

"This ain't none of your fuckin' concern. Me and my ex-wife got some shit to work out. Get in your car and go back to wherever you came from."

"Mayan, please don't leave."

"I'm not, baby," I assured her. "Damon, this the last time I'm gonna tell you to let her go."

"Nig—"

I didn't allow him to finish his sentence before my fist connected to the side of his fuckin' head. He stumbled backwards and freed Amor from his grasp. She ran off to the side as I walked over and hit his ass again. I was gonna beat him to a bloody pulp until I saw the look on Amor's face. I stopped and took a few steps back and wiped the sweat from my brow.

Seeing Damon yoking Amor up took me back to my teenage days when my pops beat my mother for sport. I don't fuck with domestic situations. My eyes found their way to Amor, and she stood there shivering with her attention focused on me and my every move. I walked over to her and placed her face in my hands.

"Are you 'ight?"

She quickly nodded her head as a lone tear fell from her eye.

"Go inside. I'll be there in a minute."

Amor nervously looked between me and Damon.

"He'll be 'ight. Go inside."

Hesitantly, Amor walked past me and went inside the house. I knew she was still by the door listening. As long as she was out of his grasp, I was cool with it.

"I don't know what business you have with Amor, but that shit is over with as of today. Don't fuckin' call her, don't come by this house, don't even fuckin' think about her! Stay the fuck away. Whatever the courts had you paying, dead that shit. My bitch doesn't need a muthafuckin' dime from you. Get yo' pussy ass off her property."

"You know what," Damon stood up and wiped blood from his nose. "Fuck her. Fuck you. I don't need *her*. She needs me. She ain't got shit going on for herself. Once she drains your pockets, she's going to come crawlin' back to me. Just wait."

Damon spit blood on the ground and wobbled to his car. It took everything in me to not go in my truck and get my gun. He wasn't worth the murder charge.

Even though he was gone, I waited another five minutes to make sure he didn't double back. When I walked inside Amor's house. She was leaning against the back of the couch with a bag of ice in her hand. She looked at me with puffy red eyes.

"What happened to him?"

"Don't worry about him. He won't be back."

 "Here put this on your hand or it's gonna swell."

"I'm good. Let me ask you something. What did you think was going to happen when you opened the door? You thought you were going to have a civil conversation with the same nigga that played you for dust?"

"Excuse me?"

"What was your fuckin' thought process?"

"Mayan you have no right!"

"I don't have a right? That nigga had you hemmed up on your fuckin' door and would have beat your ass if I hadn't come back. What were you thinking?! On top of that, I asked you if something was wrong, but you flat out told me it was all good. What the fuck you lie for? That's how you givin' it up?"

"How was I supposed to tell you my ex-husband stopped paying for the only thing I cared about? Huh? I didn't want my problems to become your problems!"

"You said '*we go together*' right? The minute you said it, every muthafuckin' problem you have becomes mine. Especially the ones dealin' with another nigga! You're *my* woman! What the fuck I look like having you deal with your ex by yourself? Shit doesn't make sense, Amor. Use your fuckin' head!"

By now, Amor was crying and rocking back and forth. Nothing productive was going to be solved tonight. Tempers were flared and my hand was starting to sting. I drew in a long-frustrated breath. I hated seeing women weak for pussy ass men who put their hands on them.

"Stop yellin' at me like I'm a fuckin' child. I know I fucked up. I didn't think he would do that. Damon's never laid a finger on me. You don't get to come in *my* house trying to check me!"

"You right," I nodded my head. "I need air. Have a good night, Amor. Lock your door."

"Mayan!" I yelled. "Don't walk away from me. Please don't do that. Don't walk away from me when things get hard. You have every right to be upset, however you don't get to act like this was on me. The only person at fault tonight is Damon!"

Mayan had a tight grip on my doorknob. I thought he was going to pull it off if he flexed one of his muscles. He placed his head on the door and drew in a sharp breath.

"Look, I ain't mean to go off on you. Seeing Damon in your face and the fear in your eyes took me back to a very dark time. I didn't mean to snap like that."

Walking over to him, I placed one hand on the back of his neck and the other around his waist and rested it on his stomach. I could feel the insane amount of tension in his body. I wanted to ease every worry flowing through him right now. Internally, I was kicking myself for allowing this situation to happen.

"Look at me," I whispered softly. "Mayan, open your eyes and look at me, baby."

Mayan unclenched his fists and rolled his shoulder to ease the tension in the back of his neck. He stood up right, before his eyes found mine. We stared at each other for what felt like an eternity. No words needed to be spoken. He was able to read my mind as I read his. Wrapping my arms around his neck, he reached down and lifted my chin. I pulled him in for a heated kiss. Seeing him protect me sent me into overdrive. No one has ever stood up and fought for me the way Mayan had just done. I was going to devour every part of this man.

Before I could act, he reached down and slipped his fingers inside my shorts. I sighed softly after feeling his fingers massaging in between my pussy lips. A pool of wetness dwelled between my thick thighs. He was only a few strokes away from bringing me to an orgasm.

"I-I think I'm falling in love with you," I panted.

"I know, baby."

Taking me by the hand, Mayan led me over to the couch.

"What are we doing?"

"Be quiet and just go with it," he fired back. "Take those shorts off and sit on the back of the couch."

"What?"

"Amor don't make me tell you again."

The look in his eyes was damn near demonic. I carefully slid my shorts down and climbed on the couch and took a seat. Mayan sat down in front of me and rested the back of his head on my stomach. I caressed his waves as he pulled in deep long breaths.

"Come here," he instructed.

"Where am I going?"

"Sit on my face. I wanna taste that pussy."

"Oh."

Lifting off the couch, Mayan helped ease me down towards his face.

"Dance, Amor," he commanded before he dove in headfirst.

I held onto the back of the couch for support as tremors of satisfaction ripped through my hardening clit. The mystical stroke of his tongue was unraveling me. He was so good at this shit, I wanted to submit to him fully, take his last name, and bare as many children as his heart desired.

"Mayan," I moaned his name. "Mayan, why are you doin' me

like this?"

"I need yo' ass to remember who the fuck I am," he responded, before removing his mouth from my aching pussy.

"Why did you stop?" I whined trying to catch my breath.

"Get up and get on your knees."

I could barely move. How the hell did he expect me to do that?

"Amor, don't—"

"I know. Don't make you repeat yourself."

Using the little energy, I had left, I got down on the plush carpet on all fours. I dipped my back into a deep arch and spread my legs for him to have easy access. The feeling of his warm lips on my ass caused me to jump.

"What you jumpin' for? You scared?"

"No," I whimpered.

"Good."

Before I could guess his next move, he was gripping my ass and pushing that addictive penis inside my opening.

"Shit, this pussy always soaked for me. Is it gonna stay like this, Amor?"

"Dammit!" I yelled, sounding like he was hurting me, but this was far from pain. This was fucking magic. *Dammit* was the only word I was able to utter. Fuck being able to answer his question. I was trying to remember how to breathe.

"Amor, this my pussy?"

"Mmmm."

"Answer the question."

SMACK! Mayan delivered a blow to my ass.

"Yesssss!"

Mayan went to work with fast and steady strokes. Each stroke felt like he was taking ownership of my mind, body, and soul. I quickly blinked out a few tears of joy.

"Fuck, Amor. Why this pussy so fuckin' good?"

"Mayan!" With each stroke, his name dripped off my lips. "I want this forever."

Me uttering those few words sent Mayan into overdrive. He quickly flipped me over on my back and placed himself back in my hole without skipping a beat. Wrapping my hands around his back, I held onto his shoulders and rode the tsunami wave to ecstasy. He looked me in the eye and grabbed a hold of my throat.

"Amor," he grunted. "I'm 'bout to cum in this pussy."

"Do it."

--

Mayan and I lay on the floor, limbs intertwined, with only a throw blanket covering our naked bodies. Soft jazz music played over the speakers and a small fire crackled under the mantle. I carefully listened to the melodious sound of his heartbeat as his fingers caressed my arm. We were engrossed in our own thoughts. My mind raced, wondering what was going to come of this relationship. Mayan was perfect in every aspect. Was this too good to be true? How did *I* get so lucky? Would I be able to treat him as well as he treats me? Was this too soon to be falling for someone? I needed answers, but I guess he did too.

"Amor."

"Hmm."

"Are you over that nigga?"

I sat up, covered my bare breasts, and focused on him.

"Absolutely. I want nothing to do with Damon. He is a thing of the past and you won't have to worry about him anymore."

A relieved looked washed over his face. I leaned down and

placed a quick peck on his lips.

"Lay back down and tell me what the facility means to you?"

"It means everything to me. When I was their age, I wished I had a safe space to dance and express myself, but my family couldn't afford to send me to those places. I knew when I was able to, I wanted to open a safe and affordable place for the girls in my old neighborhood to express themselves. It's not just an after-school activity. It's a lifestyle for them. They don't have to pay a dime. The only thing we require is a good GPA along with a few volunteer hours and they can attend as many classes as their hearts desire. I can't let that place close."

I didn't realize I was crying until he reached over and wiped my cheeks.

"It's all going to work out. You don't have to worry about it anymore."

"Mayan," I sobbed. "I can't let you take care of that. It's *my* responsibility and I have some money saved—"

"I got you Amor. If you're good to me then I'm even better to you."

He placed a kiss on my forehead before getting comfortable and falling to sleep.

Four Months Later

"Mayan and Amor, y'all need to bring your asses out here. We ain't got all day," Mo called out.

I removed my lips from Amor's neck and my hands from her ass. She jumped off the desk, smoothed her dress down and wiped lipstick off my cheek.

"You sure I can't slide in right quick?"

"No!" She shrieked. "We gotta go, Mayan. Everyone is waiting on us."

"Let me just kiss it," I damn near begged.

Her sweet scent filled the air causing my mouth to water. I wanted her. Fuck that, I *needed* her. I was addicted to Amor Daniels, and I wasn't ashamed to admit it.

The last four months have been the best I've ever experienced. She opened my heart, my eyes, and my mind. We did everything together. Ate, slept, prayed, worked out…you name it we did it. When you saw one the other wasn't far away. We still managed to have our time away from each other when we were working, but we always made our way right back into each other's arms. I couldn't have asked for a better partner.

A week after the Damon incident, we came out to the public as an official couple. To fan down the outrageous flames surrounding our relationship, Amor and I gave Diane Rose an exclusive interview she was able to put up on her blog. Of course, she tried pressing Amor about the *How to Snag a Baller* class, but Amor handled it with style and grace and even offered Diane a few pointers. I was against the interview it at first, but Amor and Maria felt it was good for our images. Especially with the rumors flying around as to why Damon had a broken nose and a black eye. He claimed it was from a sparring workout with a close friend, but most people speculated the injuries came from me. I never confirmed nor denied it. I just know that was the last time he contacted Amor.

"Mayan, if you can get through this ceremony, I promise you'll be able to have your way with me tonight."

"Is that a promise?"

"You damn right, baby," she whispered in my ear before kissing my cheek.

"Let's get this shit over with. I'm tryna have you bent over in those muthafuckin' heels."

Keeping my promise to Amor, I took over the funding of her dance studio. When I had my guys come and inspect it, there was plenty of work to be done. I paid top dollar to have it fully gutted and renovated as quickly as possible. While the construction was under way, Amor and the girls were able to dance and practice at a studio I'd rented out. Seeing her happy and worry-free while in her element was the best feeling in the world. Knowing I was the one who put the smile on her face was a fuckin' ego booster.

The work on the building was done and it was time to show the girls. Amor was going to just invite them over and have a little snack situation and such, but I wasn't fuckin' with it. This was her baby, and we were gonna do it big. I had a cater come out, a party planner set it all up, and even had a style team come and dress the girls up. Mo, being the hard-working socialite she is, had press covering the event.

"You look so handsome, Mr. Banks."

"You look better Ms. Daniels."

"Maybe, I'll keep the heels on tonight when I bend over the bed to let you hit it from the back."

"Fuck it, they can wait."

I picked Amor up, placed her against the wall as she wrapped her legs around my waist. We hungrily kissed one another as she reached down and started pushing off my suit jacket.

"Oh no the fuck you don't!" Mo barged into the office. "Put her down, right now!"

Amor giggled and tried to hide her face. It felt like we were two teenagers getting caught for sneaking around behind the school's bleachers.

"Get your freak on and work on making a baby after we open those doors."

Amor tapped me to put her down and ran into the bathroom to freshen up.

"Mayan, I love how you're treating my girl, I swear I do. But give her pussy a rest."

"Stop minding grown folks business Mahogany Monique!" Cal yelled.

"My dog," I acknowledged, holding out my hand for a dap.

"Nah, playa. I'm on her side. Give Amor's ass a rest. Out here fuckin' like rabbits and shit."

"Shut up, nigga," I chuckled.

Amor emerged from the bathroom refreshed and ready to go.

"Are you ready to open the doors to your studio, Ms. Daniels?"

"Yes, I am, Mr. Banks."

--

Our day was finally over, and Amor and I were back at my place. Shit, she practically lived here. The grand re-opening of *For the Love of Dance* studio was a success. Seeing her and the girls happy and having the time of their lives was worth every fucking penny.

"Have I thanked you yet?" Amor asked when she stepped out on my bedroom balcony.

"Yeah, about a million times, but one more won't hurt."

"What if I thanked you another way?"

Amor stood in between my legs and passed me a glass of whiskey. I raised my eyebrow when she started kneeling down. She swiped her pretty pink tongue on her top lip...then her bottom. Her amber eyes were melting my heart and stiffening my dick.

"Mr. Banks can I, have you?"

"Yeah, baby. Show me what you got," I replied, placing the glass to my lips.

Amor slithered her fingers in my shorts and pulled out my dick, massaging every inch of it. She wrapped her warm, wet mouth around the head of my dick and tightened it...teasing the tip.

"Oooooo, shit."

"Hmmm," she hummed as she slurped and sucked my dick.

She surprised me by sliding it so deep down her throat she started gagging and grinning. My woman was a fuckin' freak and I loved that nasty shit. I grabbed a fist full of her hair and pulled her up, smashing her lips into mine. Wrapping my arms around her waist, I pulled her body into mine, trying to fuse them together. On cue, she straddled me and lowered down onto me.

"This muthafucka so damn tight, Amor. Fuck!"

My words ignited a fire in her because she started bouncing up and down like she was in a fuckin' rodeo. My mouth latched onto her breast while flicking on her clit, intensifying the pleasure.

"Put those hands on the wall and ride this shit," I groaned, smacking her juicy ass.

"Yesss!" She groaned as she did what she was told.

"Whose pussy is this, Amor?"

"Yours, Mayan. Yours!"

"Whose? Call me what I like, ma."

"Yours, Mr. Banks! Fucking yours!"

"I love you, Amor. Fuck I love your ass so fuckin' much."

"I love you too, Mr. Banks."

Amor and I fucked each other harder until my chest grew tight, my vision clouded, and I could barely breathe. Sweat dripped from our bodies as we reached that familiar place of euphoria.

"I am all yours, Mr. Mayan Banks."

"And I'm yours."

The End!

OTHER TITLES BY A. GAVIN

Perfect Dreams & Hood Nightmares (Blair & Nel Book 1-3)

When Karma Comes to Collect (Book 1-2) (Karma & Manahil)

Married to the Cartel: A Perfect Dream (Blair & Nel Book 4)

Married to a Young Savage (Denim & Static Book 1-2)

Capturing the Heart of an Opp: Episode 1: Na'Zari's Story (Na'Zari & Derron)

Hustla's Holiday: Darnael & Blair (Blair & Nel Book 5)

Christmas Night with You: A Holiday Erotica (Neva & Elijah)

In My Projects: A Low-End Courts Love Story (Aja & Khalil)

Enticed by a Cartel Boss (Ani & Owen Book 1)

Killa Kam (Kamye & Kiano)

Sex & Cigarettes (Amor & Mayan Novella)

Thug's Crown & Glory Book 1 (Ni'Asia & Rafiq)